QUEEN'S GATE JUNIOR SCHOOL
125-128 QUEEN'S GATE
LONDON SW7 5LJ
TEL 0207 761 0303

Alice in Wonderland

Retold by
Susie Linn

Illustrated by
Alexandra Ball

TOP THAT

Licensed exclusively to Top That Publishing Ltd
Tide Mill Way, Woodbridge, Suffolk, IP12 1AP, UK
www.topthatpublishing.com
Copyright © 2015 Tide Mill Media
All rights reserved
2 4 6 8 9 7 5 3
Manufactured in China

Retold by Susie Linn
Illustrated by Alexandra Ball

All rights reserved. No part of this publication may be reproduced, stored in a retrieval system, or transmitted in any form or by any means, electronic, mechanical, photocopying, recording or otherwise, without the prior written permission of the publisher. Neither this book nor any part or any of the illustrations, photographs or reproductions contained in it shall be sold or disposed of otherwise than as a complete book, and any unauthorised sale of such part illustration, photograph or reproduction shall be deemed to be a breach of the publisher's copyright.

ISBN 978-1-78445-583-5

A catalogue record for this book is available from the British Library

One sunny summer's day,
Alice sat by the riverbank
feeling hot, sleepy and rather bored.
Then the strangest thing happened.

Out of nowhere, a white rabbit clutching a pocket watch
dashed past ... and disappeared down a rabbit hole!

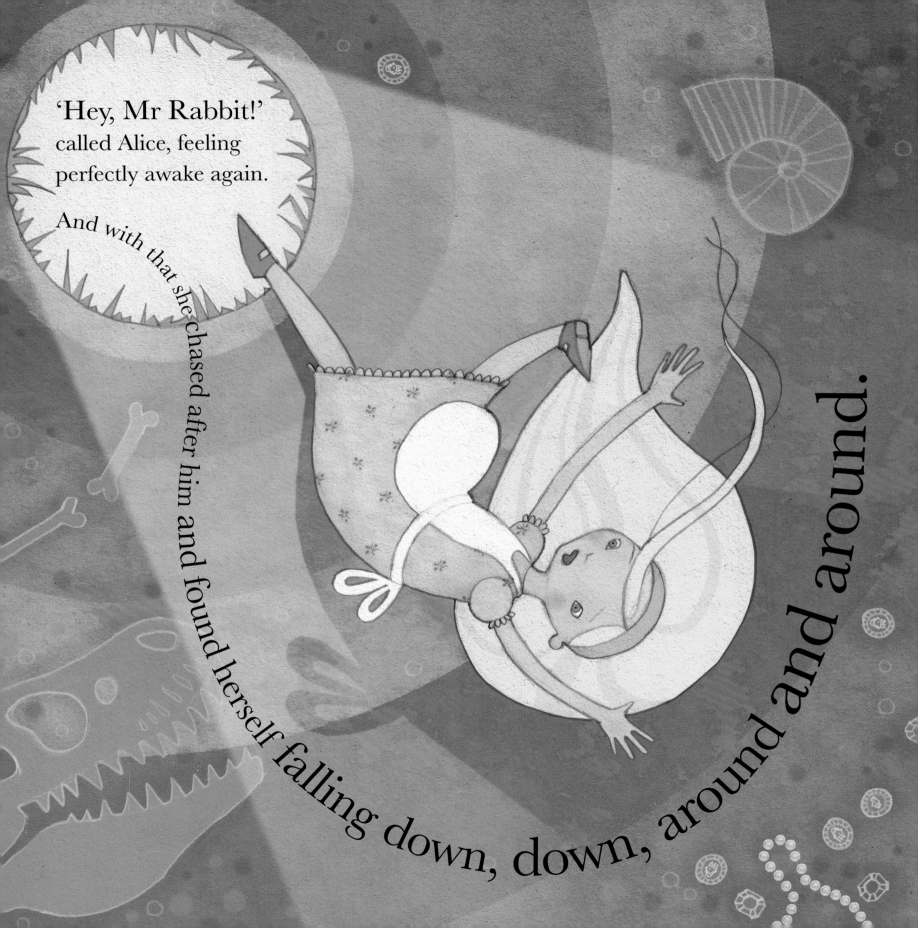

'Hey, Mr Rabbit!' called Alice, feeling perfectly awake again.

And with that she chased after him and found herself falling down, down, around and around.

Alice landed with a bump and found herself in a room surrounded by doors. She tried every single one, but they were all locked.

Then she spotted a table with a tiny key on top ... and it fitted the tiniest door. But Alice could only peep through at the beautiful garden on the other side.

'How annoying!'
she exclaimed.

Next, Alice noticed a bottle with the words *'Drink me'* on it. She took a small sip ... and shrank to a teeny-tiny size!

But she had left the key on the table, so she couldn't open the tiny door!

Drink me

'How annoying!'
exclaimed Alice again.

Then Alice spotted a cake with the words *'Eat me'* written on it. 'Mmm, why not?' she thought, taking a nibble.

And with that she grew and grew and grew SO big that her head hit the ceiling – and she started to cry. Alice cried so hard that her tears began to flood the room, opening one of the doors.

When, at last, Alice shrank again, she found herself swimming in a sea of her own tears, along with lots of other creatures. The water washed them right out of the house and Alice swam to land, to get dry.

All seemed well until,
suddenly, the White Rabbit
dashed past again.
'Where are the Duchess' gloves?'
he called to Alice, and ordered
her into a nearby cottage
to find them!

Inside, Alice started to grow again.
'Oh no!' she cried in despair,
as her arms stuck out of the windows.

The animals outside were so scared that
they threw pebbles at Alice ... and the
pebbles turned to tiny cakes!

'I might as well try one,' gulped Alice,
through more tears. And with one nibble,
she started to shrink again.

Now Alice was REALLY confused.
She ran into the woods where she
came across a big blue caterpillar
sitting on an enormous mushroom.

'Nibble one side of the mushroom to get taller,'
advised the caterpillar, wisely, 'and nibble
the other side to get smaller.'

'Yes ... why not,' said Alice.
And she experimented until she
felt about the right size again.

'What a relief!' she sighed.

It was then that Alice noticed the Cheshire Cat, sitting in a tree.

'Prrrr ... You should visit the March Hare,' said the Cheshire Cat, helpfully.

Then he disappeared ...
all except for his big grin,
which floated in the air.

So Alice went to the March Hare's house,
where there was a tea party.

'I'd LOVE a cup of tea,' said Alice,
looking at the other guests: the March Hare,
the Mad Hatter and a very sleepy dormouse.

'Here, time stands still,'
explained the Mad Hatter.

'It is ALWAYS teatime!'

The tea-party guests talked nonsense, so Alice left to explore
and came across a pretty garden. In the middle were three gardeners
in the shape of playing cards, busy painting white roses red!

'The Queen of Hearts HATES white roses!'
they muttered. 'Quick, she's coming!'

Everyone dashed to the courtroom,
and Alice was swept in with the crowd.

'The Knave of Hearts is accused
of stealing the Queen's tarts!'
announced a bossy man, to the jury.

Suddenly, a voice shouted,
'The trial is beginning!'

Alice could hardly believe it when the Queen shouted to her,
'Here! You! Come and play croquet with us!'

So Alice joined in the strangest game ever.
They played using flamingos and
hedgehogs ... and it was chaos!

And with that, a procession arrived. There were more playing cards, the King and Queen of Hearts, and the White Rabbit!

'Oooh!'

exclaimed the jury,
which was made up
entirely of creatures
great and small.

As the trial continued, Alice became more and more confused ... and more and more annoyed. She also started to grow and grow!

'Calling Alice!' shouted the bossy man.

But as Alice tried to walk through the courtroom,
she knocked over the jury box and all the animals in it!

'Off with her head!'

shrieked the Queen of Hearts.

Alice had had enough!

'You're all just a pack of cards!'

she yelled, as playing cards
flew into the air and
down over her.

At that very moment,
Alice woke up! She was by
the riverbank again, with nothing
but a few leaves falling gently over
her. It had all been a dream ... the
strangest, most amazing dream ever.

'Mmm ... time for tea!'
thought Alice, smiling to herself.